The Virgins' Treasure Isle

A true story of a huge pirate treasure

2nd Edition

The Virgins' Treasure Isle is about Norman Island, buried treasure and The Caves. It is a fascinating story of pirates against colonial masters when European nations were battling for supremacy of Caribbean islands, and omnipotent Spain was robbing silver, gold and jewels from American Indians in the name of Catholicism.

The value of the treasure the pirates absconded with in 1750 amounted to millions of pounds, perhaps as much as 20 million at today's value. It was the result of an international incident that almost brought to an end the peace that had just been concluded between England and Spain.

There are many stories of pirates and buried treasure but most of them are based on flimsy evidence. The Virgins' Treasure Isle is so intriguing because a huge portion of the treasure is still unaccounted for, and letters, documents and manuscripts surrounding the events are still in existence today.

The Great Train Robbery and the Spinks gold hi-jack pale into the shadows of this great escapade and there can be little doubt that Robert Louis Stevenson used parts of the Norman Island story for his perennial adventure, Treasure Island.

Acknowledgements

The Public Record Office in London provided much information from original manuscripts still in their possession, and Jonathan Hildreth researched some of these almost illegible documents to ferret out information. Henry Creque spent time with me going over historical facts, land titles and deeds. Michael Arneborg gave me ideas on where to look for information. The staff of the Tortola Public Record Office and the St. Thomas library were instrumental in providing assistance. Jeremy Putley spent valuable time editing the script.

Cover and pirate illustrations by Howard Pyle
"Capture of Blackbeard" by J.L.G. Ferris
Photographs by the author

The Virgins' Treasure Isle

A true story of a huge pirate treasure

2nd Edition

by

Julian Putley

Virgin Island Books

The Virgins' Treasure Isle

by
Julian Putley

Published by: Virgin Island Books
P.O. Box 8309,
Cruz Bay, St John,
US Virgin Islands 00831

e mail: putley@surfbvi.com

ISBN 0-9667923-1-9

Dedications

Dedicated to those with an adventurous spirit and the courage to search out their dreams.

Sterling Hayden was an accomplished film actor, writer, sailor and adventurer and he saw the light while sailing in the South Pacific in his traditional gaff-rigged schooner. The following is excerpted from his novel, "Voyage."

In the worship of security we fling our lives beneath the wheels of routine. We are brainwashed by our economic system until we end up in a tomb beneath a pyramid of time payments, mortgages, preposterous gadgetry and playthings that divert our attention from the sheer idiocy of the charade. The years thunder by. The dreams of youth grow dim where they lie caked on the shelves of patience. Before we know it the tomb is sealed.

When you consider the beauty there is in the world, the rapture that can be known, the honest relationships, the excitement and exaltation there is for the taking – the real things to look at and feel and read. Where, then, lies the answer? In choice. Which shall it be: bankruptcy of purse or bankruptcy of life?

"A short life and a merry one."
Motto of the ruthless pirate, Bartholomew Roberts.

"Life is what's happening while you're busy making other plans." John Lennon

Contents

Part		Page
1	Spain's Search for Gold.	9
2	The Early Pirates.	17
3	The Treasure.	45
4	The Stevenson Connection.	65

The Treasure Caves at Norman Island are perhaps the single most popular destination for visitors to the British Virgin Islands. The deep dark caves are not only eerie and full of intrigue but are surrounded by some of the finest snorkelling in the area.

Apart from the odd tale, rumour or line in an old history book little is known of the facts surrounding "The Treasure Caves" and this little book is designed to enlighten the inquisitive.

Part 1

Spain's Search for Gold

In 1492 a New World was discovered by Christopher Columbus. Lands of emerald isles rose out of a beautiful blue and turquoise sea and waving coconut palms and white sand beaches beckoned. On three sides of this tranquil sea were two continents, with the promise of great wealth.

When the banner of Spain was first planted in the New World, King Ferdinand and Queen Isabella claimed the entire hemisphere for themselves. No-one disputed their claim until the Portuguese adventurer, Pedro Alvarez Cabral touched upon the coast of Brazil. The ensuing fight for belongership was initially decided by the Pope but this was altered by the Treaty of Tordesillas in 1494 and an imaginary line of longitude was drawn which effectively gave Spain the

Fort Geronimo in Portobelo

whole of the Caribbean. To Portugal went Brazil.

Orders were spread throughout Europe that no other nation could trade in Spain's new colonies and immediately there were cries of discontent from countries like England and France. Word was circulating that gold and silver and other valuable treasures were to be had and adventurers and explorers were anxious to sail west and seek their fortunes. In 1519 the conquistador Hernando Cortes landed on the coast of Mexico and was greeted by Indians wearing gold and silver ornaments. In 1531 Francisco Pizarro entered Peru and here too the Indians were adorned in gold and silver. This overjoyed the Spaniards who had dreamed of finding precious metals in the New World. The Indians were not only peaceful but regarded these strange white men with their big cannon-bearing ships as Gods. They were easily subjugated and turned into slaves to work the gold and silver mines. Working in appalling conditions in the heat and damp of the underground mines they died in their thousands.

There were four great mining centres in the New World: Guanajuato and Zacatecas in New Spain (now Mexico) and Potosi in the old viceroyalty of Peru, now Bolivia, and Huancavelica in Peru. The silver was smelted into bars or ingots sometimes weighing as much as seventy-five pounds, the gold in seven and ten pound bars. Coins were crudely cut from these bars and often crudely struck with the Spanish coat of arms. They were considered legal tender if any part of the design showed and as long as they were of the standard weight.

At least once a year two fleets of galleons would sail from Spain to the New World. They would bring much

Vultures at Fort Geronimo

needed supplies and personnel for the burgeoning new colonies: guns, powder and shot, tools, cartwheels, equestrian tack, equipment for the mining industry, clothing, weaponry, food and wine and so on. These cumbersome, heavy, three and four deckers with huge sterncastles were armed with cannon and swivel guns and although they were slow they carried large cargoes. The two fleets had different names: one was called the Galeones or Galleons, the other was the Flota. The Flota went to Mexico and the Galleons headed for Cartagena and then on to Portobelo on the Caribbean side of the isthmus of Panama. As early as 1537 these fleets were guarded by men o' war to protect them from pirates as they sailed through the Caribbean.

When the galleons arrived at Portobelo a great trade fair was held with much revelry, drinking, singing and dancing. The ships were unloaded of their much needed cargoes and the wealth of Peru was loaded aboard from huge caches that had been stored in giant warehouses ashore. Often tons of silver was shipped up the Pacific coast from Peru to Panama and then loaded onto donkeys for the overland crossing of the isthmus to be deposited in the heavily guarded giant sheds. When the fair was over and the loading complete the galleons would head back to Cartagena for more cargo to be loaded: gold, pearls and emeralds, tobacco, vanilla, indigo and coffee from the Spanish Main.

Meanwhile the second fleet was loading its ships with the silver of Mexico at Veracruz – again the ingots of silver that the Spaniards wrested from the enslaved Indians amounted to many tons. Often the arrival of the Flota was timed to co-incide with the arrival of the Manila galleon in Acapulco; its treasure would be transported overland and loaded aboard a ship of the

Flota.

When all was ready the two fleets would sail for Havana in Cuba and prepare for the voyage to Spain. It was a hazardous voyage with the reefs and shoals of the Bahamas, and hurricanes and tropical storms in the summer months. It is surprising that these richly laden ships should have attempted such a perilous voyage in the hurricane season but this they did, time and time again. The most dangerous hazard of all was an attack by pirates and by the mid 1600s pirate lairs existed in Port Royal, Jamaica and New Providence, Bahamas – both strategically placed for raids on the Spanish fleets. Jamaica was perfectly placed to attack the Cartagena galleons headed for Havana and the New Providence (now Nassau) location was ideal for attacking the whole Armada as it sailed north up the Florida Straits before turning east for Spain.

The Author at the Gold Warehouse in Portobelo

Caravel Replica – around 1700

Part 2

The Early Pirates

Apart from the lure of huge riches there were two other major influences that encouraged piracy in the Caribbean. One was the Inquisition, an ecclesiastical doctrine for the suppression of heresy rigidly adhered to by the Spanish Catholics. The other was the arrogance of Spain in claiming all lands in, and bordering on, the Caribbean sea as Spanish territory, and the reservation of them for trade only with Spanish ships.

In the mid-16th century many Britons along with Germans, Dutch and the Huguenots of France were, for various reasons, splitting from the Catholic church. One such Protestant Briton was a Royal Naval chaplain named Drake and one of his twelve children, Francis, was to become, arguably the greatest seaman of all time, and to the Spaniards of the Caribbean, the most feared. At an early age he had witnessed shipmates being burned at the stake, put to the rack and thrown into dungeons for nothing more serious than being Protestant. His hatred of the Spaniards was to last his lifetime. Many privateering expeditions sent out by England, under such able commanders as Drake, Sir John Hawkins and Sir Richard Grenville, were accused of "Protestant piracy" by the infuriated Spanish whose ships they looted and whose towns they sacked.

In 1558 Queen Elizabeth 1st, a Protestant, ascended the throne. She regarded the Spaniards with apprehension, not only because of their Catholic fanaticism, but because their New World exploits were reaping rich rewards and Spain was becoming rich and powerful. She gave legal letters of marque to Hawkins as well as financial backing. Although the Spaniards regarded Hawkins as a pirate he was actually a privateer and smuggler of slaves. He robbed the Portuguese of their negroes on the Guinea coast of Africa and sold them to the Spaniards in the West Indies. It was on a similar voyage with a fleet of six ships, two belonging to the Queen herself, and commanded by Hawkins, that the twenty-two-year-old Drake was again influenced against the hated Spaniards. The fleet had been trading along the coast of the Spanish Main and on the homeward leg the fleet was caught by a terrible storm in the Yucatan Channel. They were blown down to a narrow bay called San Juan de Ulua and there promised safe haven by the Spaniards. An act of treachery, a surprise attack, almost cost Drake and Hawkins their lives. They managed to struggle back to England minus four ships and all their treasure.

Drake now had experience and local knowledge. His next Caribbean voyage was to Nombre de Dios, the terminus of the silver train (it later moved to Portobelo). Drake lay in wait for the arrival of the treasure which he knew was timed to co-incide with the arrival of the Galleons from Spain and his patience was rewarded. His haul on this raid on over two hundred fully laden mules was thirty tons of heavy silver bars. On his return the whole of England was ecstatic at his bold adventure and rich prize.

But the zenith of Drake's career was yet to come. Now he had finances and authenticity – all he needed to prepare for another expedition. With the Queen's backing he set out, with four small privateers, and the ship that was to be renamed the *Golden Hind.* He battled for more than two months in storm tossed seas to sail around Cape Horn in order to raid the weakly defended coastal towns of Chile, Peru and Mexico. While cruising off the west coast of South America he attacked and captured the great plate ship *Nuestra Senora de la Concepcion,* more commonly called the *Cacafuego* or Shitfire. This one ship added an incredible treasure of over four hundred thousand pesos in gold and silver to his collected loot – many millions in today's currency. Eventually she sailed westwards through the uncharted and reef strewn South Seas back to England, stopping only at the Moluccas, Java, and Sierra Leone. Two years and ten months after his departure he once again sailed into Plymouth harbour, loaded to the gunwales with treasure. It was the year 1581 when Drake was knighted by Queen Elizabeth 1st whose hesitancy was quickly overcome by a generous share of the huge treasure.

It is beyond the scope of this short story to delve

Henry Morgan in his latter years

too deeply into the exploits of this great seaman but necessary to highlight the fact that Drake was the first to seriously challenge the monopoly of the Spaniards. Whether he was pirate or prince depended on whose side you were on, and he set the stage for future events in the Caribbean.

Wars were often fought by European nations because of events that had taken place in Caribbean waters. Henry Morgan of Jamaica was the most notorious and successful pirate of all time. He arrived at Barbados as an indentured servant in 1657 and may have enlisted in the army of Penn and Venables' Jamaica expedition to obtain his freedom. From this station it was a logical step to become a soldier of fortune, privateer and pirate. In 1668 Morgan embarked on one of his early profitable raids on the treasure warehouses of Portobelo. After a rough passage across the Caribbean Morgan anchored his fleet in the roads off Portobelo and sent his men to the city in canoes. The first two garrisons surrendered without a fight being terrified by the blood curdling screams and musket fire of the attacking pirates. The third fort was not taken so easily being commanded by the governor himself declaring that he and his men would fight to the death. The walls of the impressive forts at Portobelo were not easily breached and the defenders poured fire down onto the attackers repelling them for a while. But Morgan was not to be so easily rebuffed and ordered prisoners, mostly nuns and priests, to advance forwards with ladders and place them against the walls of the fort to facilitate the pirate's access. The pirates eventually conquered the Spaniards who, along with the governor, fought to the end. Morgan returned to Port Royal, Jamaica, with two hundred and fifty thousand pieces of eight and vast quantities of valuable merchandise.

Morgan was now financially able to prepare for further raids. This he did with a raid on the rich city of Maracaibo in present day Venezuela. Whilst in Lake Maracaibo pillaging and plundering, his escape through the narrow entrance was suddenly blocked by the arrival of three Spanish men o' war. By cunning tactics he set a fire ship drifting down onto his adversaries – one ship was burned to the waterline, another ran aground and the third was captured by Morgan, who made her his flagship. He again returned to Port Royal victorious and after mild reproval from Governor Modyford was granted a new commission to prey on all Spanish ships, property and towns, in other words official permission to commit any acts of piracy he desired.

The most famous pirate raid of all time was enacted on the rich city of Panama by Morgan in 1671. The seizing of the treasures and subsequent sacking and ransom of the city would break Spain's power in the western world. In terrible conditions of heat, disease, flies and mosquitoes the pirates trekked across the isthmus of Panama. After more than twenty days of fierce battle for Panama City and the burning of a vast number of wooden buildings and the sacking of rich Catholic churches the pirates returned victorious to the Caribbean side of the isthmus of Panama. They had with them a train of 175 donkeys laden with bags of doubloons and pieces of eight; bars of gold and ingots of silver; caskets of pearls and precious stones; church plate of solid gold, encrusted with emeralds; bales of satins, silks and boxes of spices.

Morgan was greeted as a hero when he sailed back into Port Royal but his expedition had taken place when Spain and England were officially at peace. It was a sign of the times that communication took so long between the mother country and its colony. A treaty had been concluded at Madrid between Spain and England in July 1670, "restraining depredations and establishing peace" in the New World, but either Morgan chose to ignore it or had not been advised of it. Morgan was called to account and transported to England in chains for what amounted to a threat of war by Spain. But he had accumulated such riches that by suave diplomacy at Court he was knighted by King Charles 2nd. In 1674 he returned to Jamaica as governor, much to the chagrin of the Spaniards.

In order to discover how much piracy prevailed in the Virgin Islands it is necessary to look at the complete Caribbean picture. Piracy could be described as highway robbery on the high seas although much of the pillaging and plundering took place on the land. For over two centuries Spanish treasure was transported from the New World to the old on well established routes. Caribbean sources of treasure (and many riches were gathered from much further afield – the Philippines, Chile and Peru) were Chagres and Portobelo, near Panama and Veracruz and Frontera in the Bay of Campeche, Mexico. The Spanish galleons that transported the South American gold and silver usually mustered at Cartagena and then sailed on to Havana in Cuba where they would meet the treasure ships from Mexico. The whole flotilla would sail for Spain by way of the Florida Straits and then ride the Gulf Stream and the westerlies to Europe. It is naiive

Captain Kidd

indeed to think that fleets of pirate ships were lying in wait in the Virgin Islands for Spanish treasure ships – they just didn't come this way.

Despite this the Virgin Islands did have its share of colorful characters. One of the reasons was that the present US Virgin Islands was settled by the Danes (in 1672) and as such was a relatively safe refuge from the warring nations of Britain, France, Holland and Spain. Charlotte Amalie became a premier trading centre and port situated at a cross roads with the (yet to be formed) United States to the north west, Europe to the north east, and the Leewards and Windwards to the south together with the whole of the Spanish Main. Such a lucrative entrepot with its associated richly laden trading vessels could hardly fail to attract pirates.

One of the most infamous, and perhaps unfortunate, pirates of the early 18th century, William Kidd, is known to have been a visitor to Charlotte Amalie, capital of the present day US Virgin Islands. He started his career as a privateer with two commissions: one was to capture the ships of enemies of the British Crown; the other was to apprehend pirates, many of whom were in the Indian Ocean around Madagascar and were raiding rich East Indiamen with impunity.

Captain Kidd's vessel, a privateer named the *Adventure Galley* of 284 tons and mounting thirty four guns, was financed by rich sponsors and the king himself would reap a share of one tenth of the booty, in the time honoured tradition. Twenty-five per cent of everything captured went to the crew. His course was eastward toward Madagascar, a long and difficult passage in a heavy and not very weatherly ship. His crew were a motley bunch, too, made up of assorted criminals and convicts forced on him by the navy. Kidd's intentions were honorable to begin with but after disease and then the development of some leaks to the ship, rumblings of discontent and talk of "going on the account" (engaging in acts of outright piracy) were heard from the focs'le. Kidd found no enemy ships or pirates on the Madagascar coast so he sailed on to the Malabar coast of India. Here he let some richly laden Indian ships go by and finally a richly laden Dutchman. After months at sea the crew were now highly discontent, with not one prize to their name.

An inevitable altercation took place when one of the gunners swore at Kidd and in the heat of the moment the captain threw a wooden bucket at the mutinous crewman and accidentally killed him. This was the turning point in Kidd's career: whether it was the lack of success in taking prizes or a fear of being reprimanded by his backers Kidd now turned to piracy and attacked any ship, no matter what flag it flew. His greatest prize was a four hundred ton Armenian ship called the *Quedagh Merchant* loaded with a rich cargo, and Kidd decided to exchange his leaky *Adventure Galley* for the bigger and more sound ship.

Eventually Kidd returned to the Caribbean with a vast treasure, only to learn that he was a wanted man. He thought that he could explain away his piracies as Drake and Morgan had done before him. But he was mistaken: Kidd was not a popular captain and had left many abused crew and tortured villagers in his wake. Whilst in St Thomas he was refused permission to re-provision his ship and somewhere in the islands he hid vast quantities of treasure.

Some years later Kidd was hanged at Execution

Dock, London. His two original commissions that somehow disappeared during his trial and would have been evidence in his defence reappeared in the Public Record Office in London some two hundred years after his death.

There is at least one historical account that states, "The fabulous treasure of the ill-starred Captain Kidd was buried in Norman's Isle."

The most colorful pirate and perhaps the most dreaded in all pirate history was Edward Teach, Blackbeard! Like most pirates his career spanned a very short time, but was notable for its bloodthirsty encounters and excessive debauchery.

Blackbeard was born in Bristol, England and served on privateers during Queen Anne's War (1702 –1713), the base of operations being Jamaica. It is probable that when the war ended Teach moved to New Providence, (present day Nassau). Between wars seamen who had served their country on privateers were now out of work and it was natural that they should "go on the account," a term for piracy whose motto was "no prey, no pay." New Providence was a perfect location close to the main sea highway between Florida and the Bahamas. There was no law and order, the climate was good, rum was plentiful and young girls of mixed blood flocked to the place.

In 1716 Edward Teach joined up with Captain Benjamin Hornigold, the fiercest and ablest of all the pirates who regularly operated out of New Providence and one who was held in high esteem by the "Brethren of the Coast." Apparently Hornigold was impressed by Blackbeard who had, "a marksman's eye, an ability at dirty infighting and an unmatched thirst for blood."

18th century chart of the Virgin Islands, from Jefferey's West Indian Atlas.

ISLANDS

Hat I. E.
af. Dangerous Reef
61
Sunk Rock
Drake's Channel

Sombrero
or Hat I.

10

8

7
Passage b *I.*
6

5

GORDA or
ish Town E.

Salt Pond

Anguilla E

the Channel

St Martin

French Dutch Salt Pond

THE

LEEWARD

Blackbeard and Hornigold each captaining their own sloops sailed the New England coast capturing numerous prizes, most of which they scuttled after seizing and transferring the cargo. Then they headed south for the Caribbean and legend has it that Blackbeard spent time in Charlotte Amalie where a tall stone tower stands known as Blackbeard's Castle. He was a giant of a man, tall and broad with a long black beard often plaited and tied with ribbons. Before battle he was known to light hemp wicks, the same kind that were used to touch off cannon, and place these fuses under his hat with the smouldering ends protruding, to give a frightening appearance. He wore two brace of flintlock pistols from a bandolier, a dagger and a broadsword at his side.

Women and young girls were attracted to Blackbeard and his harsh demeanour softened in their presence. In fact it is said, "he became like putty in their hands." Many a harbour trollop actually proposed to Blackbeard and the fiercesome pirate often liked the idea, it being a good excuse for merriment and drunken debauchery. It is often quoted that Blackbeard had no fewer than fourteen wives.

Blackbeard may have passed through the British Virgin Islands. At Soper's Hole two off lying islands are named Thatch Island: Great Thatch and Little Thatch. These two islands are believed to be named for Edward Teach whose surname was often spelt Thatch. The anchorage off Tortola's West End was a perfect hideaway for pirate vessels. It has three access points and with a downwind getaway escape was never a problem. Careening was also possible with the steep anchorage rising to shallows on a sandy bottom next to the mangroves.

In the southern Caribbean, in November of the year 1717, and still in the company of Hornigold, Blackbeard captured the French registered ship *Concord*. A fast and strongly built Dutch three master with thirty great cannons, he transferred to this ship and renamed her the *Queen Anne's Revenge*. Then he sailed off, leaving Hornigold to his own devices, and searched for another prize. It wasn't long in coming, *The Great Allen* was a heavily armed and richly laden ship that Teach seized and forced to move close to the shore of St Vincent. Then he plundered the cargo, burnt the ship to the waterline and sank her.

A British man o' war was sent after Teach when news reached the garrison at Barbados. The thirty gun Scarborough was given orders to seek out the Queen Anne's Revenge and destroy her. The naval ship sought and found Teach's pirate ship and shot off several broadsides from long range, with little effect. But Teach had the quicker and more nimble ship and after a running battle of several hours the King's crippled ship withdrew and slowly made its way back to its station in Barbados. The mocking and jeering laughter coming from Blackbeard's crew could be heard for many cable lengths.

News of Teach's successes spread fast – after all, driving off a warship of the greatest navy in the world was no small feat. In the eyes of all the Brethren of the Coast he was invincible. But Blackbeard was as cunning as he was courageous and it seems that at about this time he set sail for Bath in North Carolina where, in January 1718 he surrendered and took an oath to give up piracy. Apparently he received a certificate of pardon on the basis of a previously issued proclamation by King George 1st. It is doubtful that he ever had any intention of adhering to his oath because at the beginning of March Teach set sail for British Honduras and on this voyage he came upon a pirate sloop commanded by Major Stede Bonnet, "a round little man in a bright waistcoat and trim breeches, clean shaven and periwigged." Teach quietly persuaded Bonnet and his ship the *Revenge* to team up with the *Queen Anne's Revenge* and together they "went on the account." Whilst in Honduras they captured the *Adventure of Jamaica* and Blackbeard put his first mate Israel Hands in command.

By the end of May Blackbeard, with a fleet of five armed ships, arrived off Charleston to blockade the port, the busiest and most important of the southern colonies. All vessels, whether inbound or outbound, were stopped; the first large vessel seized and plundered was the *Crowley*, headed for London with many of Charleston's leading citizens aboard as passengers. During a period of five or six days eight or nine vessels were seized and plundered. Blackbeard then put the town to ransom for a most unusual prize: a medicine chest! And speculation of the day raised the question that perhaps there was an epidemic of venereal disease aboard, since mercurial medicines were demanded as part of the contents of the chest.

The treasure gained from the seized ships was considerable and Blackbeard now devised a cunning method to keep it all without sharing the booty in the accepted manner. He wrecked the *Queen Anne's Revenge* at Beaufort Inlet and quietly slipped away on board the *Adventure* commanded by Israel Hands. Their hideaway was Pamlico Sound in North Carolina. Then, at nearby Bath Town, Blackbeard managed to get a pardon by yet another royal proclamation.

In September of 1718, whilst Blackbeard was enjoying "semi-retirement" from his piratical ways on board the *Adventure*, anchored at Ocracoke Inlet, his lookout spied a large brigantine and several smaller vessels approaching the inlet from the south. Blackbeard's experienced eye told him the small fleet was probably commanded by non other than the notorious pirate Charles Vane. Blackbeard sailed out to meet his fellow pirate friends from his New Providence days and eventually they all got together for a bachannal of magnificent proportions. There was cow and pig roasting, the rum punch flowed like water, and music and merrymaking lasted for several days. News, information, sea stories and scuttle-butt were swopped and eventually alarming rumours of pirate skullduggery reached Governor Spotswood of Virginia. Present at the festivities were Jack Rackham, sailing with Vane; Israel Hands; Blackbeard; and Robert Deale, along with several hundred pirates of lesser rank: the greatest collection of rogues of the deep ever to congregate on the American continent. Spotswood decided to do something about it.

In the early grey morning light on Friday, November 22nd two sloops weighed anchor and headed for Teach's hideout at Ocracoke Inlet. The pirate festival had disbanded days before but Blackbeard was there enjoying his life of retirement with a handful of less than twenty men. In command of the two vessels was Lieutenant Maynard of the Royal Navy, then an officer on the man-o'-war *Pearl*. His orders were to capture the pirate Edward Teach, dead or alive!

Blackbeard, now aboard the *Adventure* with Israel Hands, had previous knowledge of some kind of impending attack, but wrote it off as a mere nuisance. But when the pirate saw the two sloops and their continued advance, he roared across the water, "Damn you for villains, who are you?" And from whence come you?"

Then seeing that their intention was to fight he drank down a bowl of liquor and shouted, "Damnation seize my soul if I give you quarter or take any from you."

Maynard replied, "I expect no quarter from you, nor shall I give any."

Blackbeard cut his cable and elected to engage in a running battle. With local knowledge of the waterways he manouvered himself into a favorable position and fired off a broadside at his attackers and immediately disabled one sloop and killed half the men.

Maynard now employed a cunning trick – he hid most of his remaining men below decks, and when the smoke cleared Blackbeard saw nothing but dead and wounded, "They are all knocked on the head. Climb aboard and cut them to pieces," roared Teach.

One of the bloodiest and fiercest hand to hand battles ever to take place on the deck of a small ship now raged. The savagery and butchery was such that the sea around the vessel was tinctured red and the deck was slick with blood making it difficult to stand.

An excerpt from the Boston News perhaps best describes Blackbeard's end:

Teach seeing so few on the Deck, said to his Men, the Rogues were all killed except two or three, and he would go on board and kill them himself, so drawing nearer went on board, took hold of the fore sheet and made fast the Sloops; Maynard and Teach themselves then begun the fight with their Swords, Maynard making a thrust, the point of his Sword went against Teach's Cartridge Box, and bended it to the Hilt, Teach broke the Guard of it, and wounded Maynard's Fingers but did not disable him, whereupon he Jumped back, threw away his Sword and fired his Pistol, which wounded Teach. Demelt struck in between them with his Sword and cut Teach's Face pretty much; in the Interim both Companies engaged in Maynard's Sloop, one of Maynard's Men being a Highlander, engaged Teach with his broad Sword, who gave Teach a cut on the Neck, Teach saying well done Lad, the Highlander reply'd, if it be not well done, I'll do it better, with that he gave him a second stroke, which cut off his Head, laying it flat on his Shoulder, Teach's Men being about 20, and three or four Blacks were all killed in the Ingagement, excepting two carried to Virginia: Teach's body was thrown overboard, and his head put on the top of the Bowsprit. "

An informal autopsy at the end of the battle found twenty severe cuts in Blackbeard's body and five pistol shots. Maynard recognised Blackbeard as an exceptional man "superior to others in talent, in courage, in physical strength." Johnson, a pirate biographer says, "Here was the end of that courageous brute, who might have passed in the world for a hero had he been employed in a good cause."

Blackbeard was, and still is, the quintessential pirate of all times.

At the time of Blackbeard's demise Jack Rackham was quartermaster on Vane's brigantine but soon after he was elected captain by the pirate crew in the accepted fashion, Vane having been branded not sufficiently bold when he let go a prize in New

Rackham's Cay, Port Royal, Jamaica

England waters. In May 1719 "Calico Jack" as he was called, because he was prone to wearing fancy clothes, pulled into New Providence and requested a pardon from Governor Woodes Rogers. This was granted and while he was here he met the pretty wife of James Bonny, Anne. He spent a fortune on this girl with whom he had become smitten and soon his money was gone, but even so he managed to persuade her to join him. The couple returned to pirating, as so often was the case, Anne disguising herself as a man. Surprisingly, on board Rackham's ship was another female pirate, also masquerading as a man, Mary Read.

Rackham headed south and was in the process of loading the cargo of a captured and richly laden merchantman, the *Kingston,* onto his own ship when destiny changed his evil life. At the time the crew were living on a small islet or cay where they had made a temporary camp and so could not defend their ships. The governor of Jamaica had sent out two ships to capture the notorious pirates and eventually a Captain John Barret was successful in apprehending Rackham as he tried to sneak off, abandoning his crew. At his trial in Jamaica he and twelve male pirates were all found guilty and sentenced to be hanged. Official records state that they were "hung on Gibbits in Chains, for a publick Example, and to terrify others from such-like evil Practices." On the day of the executions, Anne Bonny, still in prison, said, "If he had fought like a man he need not have been hanged like a dog."

At the entrance to Kingston harbour just off Port Royal is a small cay where Calico Jack was hung in chains, his body slowly rotting away as birds pecked out

Blackbeard's Last Stand

the eyes and rats ate the putrefying flesh. To this day it is called Rackham's Cay.

At the eastern end of Tortola in the British Virgin Islands lies Trellis Bay, one of the best and most protected anchorages in the whole island group. In the middle of this bay is Bellamy Cay, named after one of the most voracious pirates in history, Black Sam Bellamy.

Bellamy was a west country Englishman who had sailed to the New England area. There he fell in love with, and made pregnant, his young cousin, Maria Hallett. Whether in spite of this, or because of it, Samuel Bellamy sailed off into the sunset in the year 1716 to go and seek his fortune. He had heard that the Spanish plate fleet had been wrecked on the Florida coast by a severe hurricane and that rich pickings were there for the taking. By the time Bellamy arrived, in his small leaky vessel, rich pickings were no longer to be had, but his career as an adventurer was about to take a giant leap forward. He met an old English pirate by the name of Ben Hornigold of the *Mary Anne* and signed on as crew. One of his shipmates, coincidentally, was none other than Edward Teach, the infamous Blackbeard. The Mary Anne sailed in company with a French ship, the sloop *Postillon*, Captain Louis Lebous. They plundered any ship they could outsail and force into submission. It seems that old Hornigold, after an encounter with three English ships, became somewhat patriotic and decreed that he would no longer plunder ships of England. This displeased the crew, who argued that their fate would be just as swift swinging from an English yardarm as from any other.

The outcome of this dissension was that Bellamy became captain. Such a meteoric rise to power in the pirate ranks says a lot for the type of man Bellamy was: brave, cunning, skillful and a good seaman with an ability to handle men.

It was not vengeance against the Spanish for their trade embargoes or the cruelty of the Inquisition that fired Bellamy, it was purely greed, and any vessel was fair game for him. He and Lebous prowled the trade lanes of the Virgin Islands capturing ship after ship and getting richer and richer. They made their base at Trellis Bay, Tortola, because it is well concealed, well protected and an excellent victualling point. Beef Island, adjacent to the bay, was so named because of the prodigious number of cattle that were reared there.

Bellamy always longed for a larger and faster vessel and near Saba they caught and kept the ship *Sultana*, a large ship with more the lines of a man o' war. He gave his first mate the *Mary Anne* and off they went, three ships now, a pirating once more.

It was in 1717, in February, that Captain Bellamy spotted the ship of his dreams – an 18 gun, 300 ton, sleekly designed sailing galley, a slave ship from the Gold Coast of West Africa, the *Whydah*. Named for the bustling slave port of her origin she looked every inch the prize flagship that Bellamy itched to own. It took three days of dogged cat-and-mouse before the *Whydah* finally rounded into the wind and hove to, surrendering. Bellamy and crew loaded all their considerable riches into the *Whydah* which now carried between twenty thousand pounds and thirty thousand pounds of gold and silver all stowed in bags and packed in wooden treasure chests. Other valuables included gold and silver jewelry and several sets of navigational instruments.

They had plundered between forty and fifty ships when, for some obscure reason, perhaps for the love or lust for the ravishingly beautiful, dark haired Maria Hallett, Bellamy turned north and headed for his New England home at Wellfleet.

In April 1717 the richest pirate ship of all time was caught in the teeth of a major storm, and on a treacherous, shoal-ridden Cape Cod lee shore, ran aground, dismasted and pounded to bits. All the pirate crew perished except for two, who lived to tell the tale. Black Sam Bellamy was no more.

The *Whydah*, with its millions of dollars worth of treasure has only recently been found. In 1985 the wreck of the *Whydah* was positively identified when the bronze ship's bell was raised. Inscribed on the side were the words, *Whydah Galley, 1717*.

If the sea lanes of the Virgin Islands were stalked by ruthless pirates it is also fair to say that the inhabitants of some of the islands were out for lucrative gain from those unfortunate enough to be found helpless at sea, and by this I mean the victims of shipwreck.

Anegada is a low flat island almost surrounded by treacherous reefs. It lies to the west of the dangerous Anegada passage, often with a strong current setting onto it. It has become the graveyard of hundreds of ships.

According to a journalist by the name of Schomburgk, who wrote about Anegada in the 1832 Royal Geographical Society journal, the first settlers came because they had noted the frequent shipwrecks and had "hopes of advantage to those who might be in the neighbourhood to profit by them. The object always was, and still is, the wreck of vessels, and the indolence of the inhabitants is only thoroughly aroused by the cry of 'a vessel on the reef!' Scarcely is the news announced than boats of every description, shallops and sailing vessels, are pushed off with all haste to the scene of action; arms which have been idle for weeks are brought into exercise and both skill and intrepidity are tasked to the uttermost to get first on board. The scene, indeed, baffles description; and it is to be feared that few are attracted by motives of humanity."

Obviously many of the early settlers of Anegada were of a base character that contrasted sharply with other Virgin Islanders of the time who were Quakers of a high moral fibre. Most of the wreckers and beachcombers of Anegada who, for some reason or other, found themselves "on the beach" were pirates, and as such originated from all walks of life and all levels of society. Many had been cruelly used and abused in an age where torture, beheadings and burning at the stake were everyday occurrences. The pirates all had one thing in common though – they were all running from society: some were escapees from cruel servitude, some were convicts and others were military men laid off between wars. By their very make-up they would not be likely to show compassion, and woe betide a vessel unfortunate enough to come to grief on the reefs of Anegada.

In an early record of deeds it states that a certain George Norman, in the year 1747, was "Grantor or Lessor of one fourth part of one seventh of the island of Anegada." Whether he was pirate, privateer, wrecker or beachcomber is not known but somehow he bought this substantial portion of Anegada. It is believed that this same Norman acquired and gave his name to the island of our story which was often referred to as Norman's Retreat. Anegada was so full of rogues that a retreat would have been a most handy asset.

Part 3

The Treasure

On the 18th of August, 1750, a fleet of ships raised their anchors and departed the port of Havana in Cuba bound for Spain. The ships that made up this fleet were: the *Nuestra Senora de Guadelupe*, a galleon captained by the fleet commander Juan Manuel de Bonilla; the *Nuestra Senora de los Godos*, a galleon commanded by Don Pedro Pumarojo; His Majesty's Ship *La Galga* captained by Don Daniel Huony; a frigate captained by Don Joseph Rospaldiza; His Majesty's Ship La Zumaca; and a packet of Portuguese registry.

The *Guadelupe* had originated its voyage in Vera Cruz and was full of silver. The *Godos*, accompanied by the frigate, had come from Cartagena and was full of assorted treasure. *La Zumaca* was laden at Havana. The treasure of the combined fleet was well into the hundreds of millions of dollars at today's values. It must have been a wary crew that sailed north eastwards between the Bahama banks and the Florida coast, but once they were clear of Grand Bahama and the one time pirates' nest of New Providence they must have breathed easier. It was a relatively simple matter to ride the gulf stream north and then to sail with the prevailing westerlies back to Europe. But as so often happens at sea when one relaxes one's vigilance it is suddenly put to the test.

On the fifth day of the voyage the fleet, all in sight of each other, were clear of the Bahamas when the sky darkened and the wind slowly backed. A fierce storm was brewing and at some stage it must have occurred to Bonilla that this was not a front but a dangerous tropical storm. They were at the latitude of 28 degrees and 51 minutes and as the wind backed the heavy and not very weatherly ships could point no better than north, north east. The east coast of America presented the fleet with a dreaded lee shore. The storm continued for days – the rain poured, lightening flashed and the wind tore at the rigging, driving the ships, now separated, inexorably towards the coast. On the 29th of August the storm increased to a hurricane and the exhausted crew of the *Guadelupe* were powerless against such a tempest. The four pumps aboard the ship were just able to keep up with the seawater coming aboard but the masts were all torn down by the ferocity of the wind and the ship had lost her rudder. The helpless vessel, now at the mercy of the howling winds and huge seas drifted into soundings near Cape Hatteras and there the crew managed to set two anchors that held the ship and saved her from wrecking. By the 31st August the stricken vessel had drifted north almost 400 miles and now lay at anchor near 35 degrees north. The next day the storm abated although the huge breaking seas threatened the vessel every minute.

The exhausted crew of the unlucky galleon now decided that their best hope for survival was to run the ship ashore. They had lost confidence in their captain, Bonilla, and were doubtful that they would get paid for the voyage, the ship now being useless. They started throwing sails and rigging overboard to prevent the ship from ever being sea worthy again and they smashed to pieces the ship's boat. Bonilla threw up his arms in despair at the stupidity of the crew and told them it would be impossible to run the ship ashore because of the numerous shoals between them and the coast. Besides, his main priority was to safeguard the valuable cargo. To this end he made his second mistake and promised the crew double wages if they changed their attitude and expended their energies in preserving the cargo and minding the passengers. Unfortunately insubordination is not helped by stroking the crew with praise and promises. In fact it is far less effective than severe punishment.

The following morning Bonilla gave orders for the pinnace to be hauled down and a crewman to reconnoitre the coast. On their return they reported the sighting of cattle tracks so Bonilla decided to investigate further. He took with him an English speaking crewman who explored the area for two days before returning with good news. They were only 5 leagues (15 miles) from the Road of Ocracoke and with skillful pilotage they could navigate the shallow and shifting banks to a safe anchorage. Bonilla found and bought a packet boat to tow the galleon and he hired a skilled local pilot. Before attempting to move the ship, though, he ordered all the cargo to be taken ashore for safekeeping, but again he ran into problems: the crew loaded no more than 50 chests of silver when they decided to revolt, armed themselves from the ship's gunroom, and demanded payment. They could not see all that silver leaving the ship without themselves being paid. Bonilla demurred but agreed to pay them their wages, but only after the reluctant sailors had unloaded all of the silver. The crew, led on by the mate, demanded a hundred dollars per man, more than was their due: again Bonilla agreed. Still not satisfied the crew now broke into the passengers' trunks with axes and stole jewelry and other valuables and abused some female passengers.

Bonilla now decided to bring the ship with the remainder of the lading to the road at Ocracoke with the help of the "Pilot of the Barr." This was finally accomplished by means of the newly acquired packet during a spell of fair weather. The mate, though, was still being intransigent and cut the cables rather than bring the anchors aboard. Then during the three days it took to bring the ship to the anchorage a snow came alongside one night and robbed a portion of the cargo and opened some chests containing letters.

Finally with the help of some Englishmen all the treasure along with the considerable cargo was taken ashore and stored in the Customs House. Bonilla now paid his crew their demands and many of them departed on an English snow. By this time some other Englishmen were laughing and mocking the unfortunate Bonilla for his inability to control his men.

But he managed to persuade some crew members to stay and act as watchkeepers over the landed cargo. It was just as well he did because one night a raid almost cost him his treasure. A band of opportunist Englishmen, with no love for Spaniards, rushed the guardroom and managed to seize some arms, almost overpowering the watch. The Spaniards gained the upper hand but Bonilla was now in no doubt of the fragility of his position. He ordered all the silver and cochineal to be returned to the crippled ship, now somewhat precariously moored in the Ocracoke roadstead and all the remaining Spaniards to guard the treasure with diligence. There were still arms on board and fifteen mounted cannon.

Bonilla now received word that the La Galga had been forced by the storm to anchor off the coast of Virginia and he immediately sent his chief pilot with letters to the captain, Don Daniel Huony, explaining his plight. At the same time he wrote to the captain general of the province asking for assistance and vessels to transport his treasure and cargo there and then onwards to Spain.

After some time a representative of the governor, an "officer of distinction" arrived by sloop at Ocracoke and impressed Bonilla that he would do all in his power to assist him but that he must accompany him to the port of Cape Fear "on account of some matters of great consequence." Bonilla agreed and arranged to load part of the treasure and effects onto the sloop. But then a further problem arose: the weather deteriorated and became very rough again. The crippled galleon was moored in shallow water – aground and pounding on the bottom at low tide, to such an extent that Bonilla feared that a main plank might spring and sink

Bilander

the vessel. Two bilanders had recently sailed into port manned by some Englishmen and, after making arrangements to hire the vessels, Bonilla decided to load treasure and cargo from the galleon onto the bilanders for safe keeping and eventual passage to Virginia. Bonilla, at this stage, was somewhat wary of Englishmen on this part of the coast but he was running out of options. He decided to put on board the bilanders a greater number of Spaniards than there were Englishmen and he told his mate to remove the sails from both vessels to render them immobile. Then he left on the sloop with the English officer to find the rest of his fleet and make arrangements for his treasure.

If things could go from bad to worse for Bonilla they certainly did when he arrived at the port at Cape Fear. The King's attorney general informed him that a tax was due on the landed treasure – ten per cent of the total was demanded. Bonilla demurred saying that it was an act of God that had driven him ashore and that he never had any intention of coming to trade. The arguing went on and eventually six and a half per cent was arrived at with Bonilla in total disagreement but being in no position to resist. He later wrote to his superior in Spain, the Marquis of Ensenada, that "making use of an absolute power they have taken out the said contribution without my having consented thereto in any manner whatever." Little did he know that these events were to be the least of his worries.

Whilst the rankling over dues was in progress a courier from the captain general of South Carolina arrived with dispatches to confiscate the effects of the ship as compensation for prizes taken by the governor of Havana since the peace treaty between England and

Snow

Spain had been signed. To add weight to the dispatches five captains who had arrived in the port complained of these same injustices saying that prizes had been made of no less than sixteen ships. Justice was not only required it was mandatory and orders were sent up to Virginia to confiscate the cargo and treasure of the *Los Godos*, the galleon commanded by Don Pedro Pumarojo, also anchored off the Virginia coast as a result of the storm.

Back at Ocracoke more derring-do was afoot. The Englishmen on board the two bilanders had resisted the Spanish mate's attempt to remove the sails. The bilanders, one owned by a Boston man called Wade and the other by a New York man, had now been hired out to the Spanish captain. Both owners, together with Owen Lloyd, plotted with William Blackstock, a seaman, to sail away with the laden vessels and it was agreed that the above mentioned owners would stay out of sight below decks. Since now Bonilla had left with the English officer and no-one with great authority remained Blackstock, who at first thought the idea of such an audacious piracy was a joke, concurred when he became convinced how easy it would be: Owen Lloyd had spent time in the Caribbean and was familiar with the waters. The small and barren island of St Bartholemew was to be their destination

They were still tied alongside the galleon from which they had been loaded with the treasure, and on a fine and windy day, October 9th, 1750, they cut the hawsers, quickly hoisted the sails, and headed for the open sea. John Lloyd, hampered by a wooden leg, was master of one of the vessels with a crew of nine, and he soon ran aground on the shoals and was caught by some Spaniards who gave chase in a rowing pinnace.

The other vessel captained by brother Owen Lloyd got clean away and was soon hull down over the horizon. On board this vessel was a total complement of fourteen: Wade; Lloyd; Blackstock; Trivet, the mate; James Moorhouse; William Damas and an old man who went by the name of Charles, and seven others.

Even though Lloyd was a good seaman and navigator it was Virgin Gorda (then called Spanish Town) that first hove into view. They sailed by the island and then came up with St Croix which Lloyd recognised. With his position firmly established he set a course to Norman Island, "one of the keys or little islands near Tortola and uninhabited, as a proper place to share their booty."

When the bilander was anchored at Norman Island they took stock of their loot. There were 55 chests of silver dollars – in each chest were three bags containing a thousand dollars so a total of 165,000 dollars was tallied. There were two chests measuring three feet in length, two feet wide and one and a half feet deep. These were filled with church plate and wrought silver. Other valuable cargo included 120 bales of cochineal each weighing about 230 pounds, 17 bags of indigo, 3 bags of vanilla, 60 bags of stems of tobacco, 86 tanned skins and 371 hides in the hair.

The silver was divided in the following manner: five chests to Lloyd, five chests to Wade and the remaining 45 chests were divided equally making almost four chests per man. Almost all the chests of silver were removed from the vessel and taken ashore and buried. Lloyd and Wade kept one chest each on board and James Moorhouse kept all of his share on board too. So a total of forty four chests were buried on Norman Island.

Blackstock now resolved to depart the bilander, having been treated badly by Lloyd on the voyage, and Damas and Charles left the ship with him. A small portion of the cargo was off loaded as well, being their share: two bags of indigo, some tobacco and twenty bags of cochineal.

Whilst Blackstock was ashore burying his loot a man called Thomas Wallis approached the bilander and enquired why the vessel had not cleared in at the port of Road Town. Lloyd replied that they had pulled in temporarily to stop a leak. When Wallis left, Lloyd, Wade and the remaining crew weighed anchor and sailed down to St Thomas.

The three pirates, Blackstock, Damas and Charles, were now in a quandary. They were on an uninhabited barren island with a fortune in loot and nowhere to spend it. Blackstock decided to go with Wallis in his cobbe to Road Town in Tortola while Charles remained to guard the booty. There Blackstock told the president of the council, Mr Chalwell, that they had landed a cargo, salvaged from a wreck in Carolina, on Norman Island, but made no mention of the silver. He explained that the tobacco was useless, having been ruined on the voyage.

Next day Chalwell decided to go over to the island to investigate and found the tobacco to be spoiled just as Blackstock had said. He then went to another part of the bay and found Charles who was guarding the cochineal. Also, to his surprise, he found several other people there digging up bags of silver dollars. He then said to the old man, Charles, that if he had any silver he had better give it to him for safe keeping because he thought the diggers would otherwise murder him. By this veiled threat and coercion Charles agreed and

Church Plate

showed Chalwell six bags of dollars that he had spent all night guarding. The next day the president of the council took the silver back to Tortola.

Soon after, a shallop sailed into the bay from St Christopher's, Captain Purser as master. Chalwell used this vessel to transport the cochineal to Tortola as well as three more bags of dollars that Charles had found. The cochineal was divided up in Tortola with a Mr John Pickering paying one hundred pounds currency per bag for ten bags.

In the meantime the diggers had found vast quantities of buried silver: Mr Chalwell, the president's son, had twenty bags; Haynes, the marshal, had thirty and a Mrs Jeff had a "considerable amount" of dollars and plate.

Realizing the game was up Damas decided to buy the shallop from Purser for one bag of dollars and tried to get clearance papers for North Carolina. Chalwell at first refused to give the vessel the necessary departure papers but finally, after the council assented, gave him "clearance in ballast" for the English colony. The shallop with Captain Purser, Blackstock, Damas and a crew of two then sailed to St Eustatius where they learned that Lloyd had been captured and was in custody.

The pirates made a quick departure and sailed to Anguilla, but word of their adventures had preceded them. Whilst ashore on a spending spree they were apprehended by Governor Gumbs.

Meanwhile Owen Lloyd and the other pirates had arrived in St Thomas in the bilander. Lloyd was now on the run. His brother John who had been master of the second bilander before he was captured off North Carolina, knew of Owen Lloyd's familiarity with the

Caribbean islands and that he was, in fact, married to a woman, a Mrs Caines of Deep Bay, from St Christopher's. Not only that but Lloyd must have been worried that the pirates who had disembarked at Norman Island, on less than cordial terms, might inform on him.

Lloyd was not wrong to be apprehensive. Bonilla was incensed by the betrayal of these Englishmen and sent out two snows from Ocracoke to search the coast, both north and south, in all the roads, ports and creeks, to find the bilander. He also sent out notices and warrants far and wide to assist in the apprehension of the felons and if all failed he swore to search the coasts of the Orinoco, the Dutch islands and St Thomas.

His perseverance and astute enquiries worked. In St Thomas, Lloyd had hurriedly left the bilander, still loaded with a large quantity of cochineal, indigo and vanilla and bought a sloop. Then he sailed to St. Croix and swopped the sloop for yet another vessel which he sailed to St Eustatius where word of his piracy had preceded him and on November 15th he was apprehended.

On the 22nd November, Gilbert Fleming, Lieutenant Governor of the Leeward Islands, whose authority included the territory now known as the British Virgin Islands, embarked and sailed from Antigua, the seat of power, to Norman Island. He had on board "two companys" the best officers and the best men of a regiment that now looks as well dressed and as fit for service as most in England." Fleming, in fact, sailed first to St Christopher's for intelligence and to post notices of a proclamation for apprehending the remaining pirates. There he met the deputy governor of Anguilla, who showed him some of the silver dollars he had wrested from Blackstock. Fleming, along with Gumbs decided to sail up to Anguilla and there he took the prisoner, Blackstock, on board the ship to interrogate him en route to Tortola.

When Fleming arrived in Tortola he had extracted almost the complete story from Blackstock and he had high hopes of retrieving the treasure. He soon found out, however, that the Tortolians had agreed not to divulge the whereabouts of the loot. Fleming had to think again and finally, believing that force would only make a tighter bond amongst the finders, decided that a method of "mildness with resolution" would be more likely to meet with success. It was Chalwell, though, who eventually suggested that an incentive such as a salvage fee might pry loose some of the loot. This had some positive effect and a few of the finders came forward after it was announced that one third would be their legal share.

The next day Fleming posted a proclamation under pain of prosecution and this, along with the agreed salvage fee, brought forth $20,429 in silver dollars and some cochineal, indigo, and hides, the people being allowed to retain $7,514.00. He also learned of Lloyd's fleeing to St Thomas and what now was in the hands of the governor of the Danish island. Not only that, but a few days prior to Fleming's arrival Governor Heilegger of St Eustatius with an armed sloop and a contingent of soldiers had sailed into Norman Island and retrieved some of the effects. Fleming reported that he would seize this foreign flag vessel if he could since no permission had been granted for entry into British dominions or for the search for treasure. Unfortunately he was too late.

Although Fleming had agreed with Chalwell's suggestion of a salvage fee he was furious at his conduct, regarding his actions as bribery, and wrote in a dispatch that he had failed in his duty and even shared in the cash himself. "His conduct disqualified him for the administration here, and it will be some satisfaction to the Spaniards, I suspended him, and left the care of the island and the execution of what I can't stay to do myself to Mr Hodges, the next in the council, who is a more capable man, and of great fortune, probity, resolution and temper."

He also noted that the landholders of Norman Island were claiming part of the treasure as were some victims of Spanish confiscations. There were grievances against the Spaniards for injustices and injuries done to the poor people of Tortola and Virgin Gorda, as explained in the dispatch to England, "the cutting of fustick and other wood at Crab Island (Vieques), in this Government, is a help to them, without which they can't subsist, and the Spaniards have lately infested this island, and the sea about it and seized several of their little vessels, and carried them into Porto Rico." There was certainly no love for the Spaniards amongst the reticent population of Tortola.

From an original treasure of almost $200,000 about $180,000 was unaccounted for. Of course there were many avenues that treasure could have disappeared down since its demise on the beach at South Carolina on the 15th of August. There were many who thought that there was still treasure secreted on Norman Island and many who thought that there was treasure that had been found but not admitted to during Fleming's official enquiries. Ever since 1750 intrigue has surrounded Norman Island.

The Treasure Cave, Norman Island

Traditional gaff ketch, "Breath" at the Treasure Caves

And what became of the pirates? We know little of their future circumstances. It could be imagined that Blackstock got off lightly after turning King's evidence. The master-mind, Owen Lloyd, didn't stay long in prison in St Eustatius. It could be that he traded information or silver for his freedom for we have heard that the Dutch governor, Heilegger, on a clandestine trip to Norman Island, succeeded in retrieving some treasure and cargo. In June, Lloyd was a free man and a burgher (protected citizen) in the Danish island of St Thomas.

It is interesting to note that in a report of the export trade between the British Virgin Islands and Britain the year 1750 saw the value of exports rise to $24,838, more than three times previous years' values, and subsequent years were also less than half that value

In the ensuing 250 years many attempts have been made to recover hidden treasure. At one time a Norman Island Treasure Company was formed, as proved in the voluminous folios of a prospectus "to bring ample returns," and parts of the landscape were blown up – nothing was found. The story was probably, at least partly the basis for Robert Louis Stevenson's Treasure Island although he used sundry bits and pieces from other tales to spice his story.

In 1893 or thereabouts a Mr H.O. Creque, a Tortola native and St Thomas businessman bought Norman Island with the view to establishing a coaling station there. A long jetty was constructed in The Bight and overtures were made by a German steamship company to buy the island. Apparently Mr Creque "has erected a house and employs a considerable amount of labour working up the island, which he terms Liberty Island."

On the leeward side of the south western promontory of The Bight there are several caves in the cliff that are accessible from the water. The southern most one has rough, natural steps carved into one side and it was at the top of these steps that, in 1910 or thereabouts, a treasure chest was found containing Spanish coins. The find was verified by a fisherman, who, whilst sheltering from the rain, found an empty treasure chest and a few telltale coins that had rolled out of range of the digger's lantern.

The promontory on today's chart is called Treasure Point, the bay to the south is Privateer Bay and much further to the east on the southern shore is Money Bay – all hauntingly reminiscent of long-gone derring-do.

Part 4

The Stevenson Connection

One of the most famous children's books ever written is Treasure Island and there has been much speculation as to the location of the island, there being many places to claim the locale, from the Bay of Honduras to islands in the Pacific. However when one looks at the facts Norman Island comes out a clear favorite.

The tale is such to delight even the most jaded reader with blind beggars, salt encrusted pirates, a treasure map and an expedition to find a Caribbean island. There's a mutiny; a cunning, wooden-legged pirate complete with parrot; a stockade; a pirate schooner; a battle; a skeleton; and finally a huge treasure interred in a cave by a maroon. As in any good

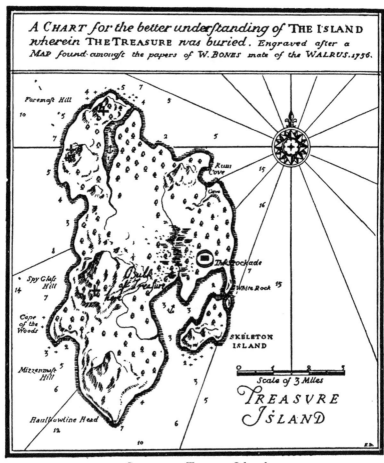

Stevensons Treasure Island

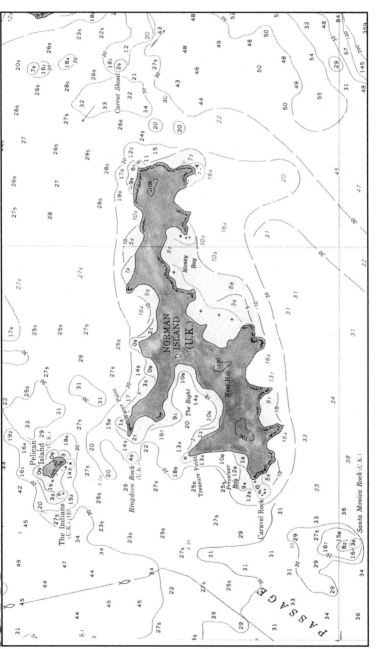

Norman Island

schoolboy yarn the good guys sail away with the treasure but the charismatic old pirate doesn't fare too badly and escapes to do battle again another day.

The story caught the imagination of the world and plays, musicals and pantomime are still annual occurrences.

There is no evidence to suggest that Stevenson ever visited the Virgin Islands but it is known that his forebears came to the islands in the latter decades of the 1700s, not long after the Norman Island treasure episode. There were two brothers, one of whom was Alan Stevenson, his great grandfather, the other a great uncle. They were involved in a trading enterprise based on the island of St Christopher's (St. Kitts), and owned a large sailing ship, a painting of which is still in the family today*. In a recorded incident that led to the death of the two brothers, both in their twenties, they pursued a corrupt agent from island to island in an open boat, "were exposed to the pernicious dews of the tropics, and simultaneously struck down." They both contracted a fever and died within 6 weeks of each other in 1774.

It seems highly likely that the story of Lloyd's huge heist and subsequent escapade would have circulated around the islands for years, particularly since Lloyd was from St. Kitts, but it can only be speculated upon whether word of the adventure reached R.L. Stevenson all those years later. It appears probable that it did.

Stevenson had a vivid imagination but he drew on past events, place names, circumstances and people to mould his story, as indeed do all writers. One of the islands or small cays in the British Virgins is called Dead Chest and the popular refrain in Treasure

Island mentions it. The famous fragment of pirate song is:

"Fifteen men on the dead man's chest,
Yo-ho-ho and a bottle of rum!
Drink and the devil had done for the rest,
Yo-ho-ho and a bottle of rum!"

The most compelling evidence that the island of Stevenson's tale was in fact Norman Island is in the treasure map. Inscribed at the bottom are the words "Treasure Island, Aug 1750: J.F.," the exact month and year of the actual piracy. And although the map of Treasure Island may have sprung partly from Stevenson's imagination it is uncanny just how similar it is to Norman Island. In fact the topography of the actual island and the fictional version would appear to be too closely related to be accidental and a comparison of the maps shown bares this out. Stevenson was highly map-minded, maintaining that a high-detail chart was better reading than most books.

In Treasure Island the fictional captain who had prior knowledge of the treasure was one J. Flint and his mate was Billy Bones. When Bones suddenly died of "apoplexy" a search was made of his sea chest and some papers and the treasure map were found. The co-ordinates for Treasure Island were given as 61° 17' 20" W, 19° 02' 40" N, less than 150 miles from Norman Island. Interestingly there is a Bone's Bay on Anegada named after an actual Anegada pirate.

Stevenson, while Treasure Island was in its genesis, asked a friend, Henley, for "a sound work on pirates for background." On another occasion he referred to Long John Silver as "a good, third-rate part-creation."

Part creation, perhaps, because a wooden-legged pirate named John was a protagonist in the real piracy.

Stevenson borrowed the name of Blackbeard's gunner, Israel Hands and used it for his mutineer cox'n. Ben Gunn, the maroon, was likely borrowed from Defoe's Robinson Crusoe. The apple barrel incident on board the Hispaniola was taken from a real life situation experienced by his father.

In the end it is only academic to analyse where all the bits and pieces came from that eventually triumphed with Treasure Island. And regardless of where all his ingredients came from Treasure Island is a masterpiece of adventure, story-writing.

END

* Stevenson wrote of this oil painting of the family's trading ship in his biographical work, "Records of a Family of Engineers." R.L. Stevenson. Chatto and Windus. 1912 book

The following letter appears to be mostly circumstantial, but parts of it are very interesting and pertain directly to the dispersal of the treasure. It is from the administrator of St. Kitts to Governor Fleming. (spelling, grammar and punctuation as in the original).

Honoured Sir,
      St. Christopher's Nov 17th, 1750

I have just now learn't the following peice of news relating to the Spanish Vessels wreck't on the Coasts of Virginia and Carolina; It seems the President of Santo Domingo with his family and fortune was on board one of them, and the ship being thought incapable of proceeding; he applied to the Governor of Carolina to assist him in hiring a vessel to carry him and his effects to Spain; the Governor could procure nothing better than a large sloop, on which the President ship't three hundred thousand peices of eight, with jewels, gold etc to the amount of two hundred thousand pounds sterling; but a few days before the sloop was to sail, one Lloyd (who married a daughter of the late Charles Caines at Deep Bay) and several other villains enter'd into a conspiracy together, run away with her and brought her to Santa Croix; there they disposed of some of the money, but not knowing what to do with so large a treasure, they buried the bulk of it in Norman's Island,(which belongs to the heirs of the late Coll: Shipps) till they could with more safety and convenience, dispose of it; Lloyd, and some of his confederates, came up to St. Eustatius two or three days ago, where the Governor of Carolina had taken care to send a proper information of their conduct, and as soon as they landed they were seiz'd and put into the Cistern; the people of Tortola got intelligence of the money buried, and have made a fine harvest of it, tis said John Hynda dug up 40,000 ps of 8, Robt Hackell 30,000, Mrs Purcell 20,000, and Mrs Jeff two canoe loads; besides jewels and plate; I thought it my Duty to acquaint your Honr. of this most flagrant peice of wickedness, that you may take such measures, and give such orders as you think proper for doing national justice upon the occasion; I presume you will think no time should be lost in securing as much of the treasure as can be, tho I fear t'will be a difficult matter to wrest it out of the hands of such people, for I believe some of em, if they can find a sanctuary elsewhere, will rather desert with it, than refund; and I hear the president himself, instead of doing his utmost to secure it, is a considerable sharer in the spoil; I am told Lloyd sent two barrels of Dollars up to his wife in this island, and I have applied to Mr Wilson, as Judge of the Admiralty to issue his warrant for seizing it.

All under this roof join in best compliments to Mrs Fleming.

Y Hon'rs Most Obed. humble Servt.
Ralph Payne.

Proclamation

Part of a Proclamation to the people of Tortola in order to retrieve the treasure and apprehend the pirates

Under my hand and Seal
at Arms this Twenty Fourth day of
November In the Twenty Fourth year
of His Majesty's Reign and in the
Year of our Lord 1750.

In the name and on behalf of His Majesty
George the Second, by the Grace of God of
Great Britain, xxx and Ireland, King, Defender
of the Faith etc
By the Hon. Gilbert Fleming Esq. Lieutenant
General and Commander in Chief of all His Majesty's
Leeward and Charibbee Islands in America.

A Proclamation:

Whereas Information has been given to me, the said Lieutenant General of a certain piracy and felony comitted on the High Seas by Owen Lloyd, William Damas, William Blackstock and others their accomplices in seizing, running away with, and converting to their own use, a Certain Sloop from North Carolina with a Treasure onboard the same Sloop consisting of Gold, Silver, Jewels, and other valuables to the value of one hundred and Fifty Thousand pounds lawful money of Great Britain or thereabouts, which sloop was hired at Carolina by the Governor of Mexico to carry the same

Treasure from North Carolina to Old Spain, on account of the said Governor, or other subjects of Spain, and that after the same Piratical and Felonious taking, the Criminals conveyd the same Sloop and Treasure to a certain little Island calld Norman Island under the dominion of His Majesty of Great Britain and within the Limits of my Goverment and there buried or conceald great part of the said Treasure and that certain British Subjects getting knowledge where the xxx Treasure lay buried, or hid have jointly and clandestinely dug up and taken and conveyd away the same to a very great value and conceal and convert the same to their own use; And whereas I the said Lieutenant General thinking myself bound by all the Tyes of Duty to my Royal Master, the King of Great Britain (whose burden it carries to have National Justice done in this and such like cases within his Dominions) to the utmost in my power to secure and bring to Justice the said Pirates and Felons and to procure the said Treasure.

Bibliography

"Treasure Island" by Robert Louis Stevenson

"The Life of Francis Drake" by A.E.W. Mason. Pub. Hodder and Stroughton. 1941

"The Buccaneer King" by Dudley Pope. Pub. Dodd, Mead & Co. 1978

"Pirates of the Spanish Main" by H. Cochran and R. Nesmith. Pub. American Heritage Publishing Co., Inc. New York. 1961

"Sunken Treasure" by Robert F. Burgess. Pub. Dodd, Mead & Co. 1988

"Blackbeard the Pirate" by Robert E. Lee. Pub. John F. Blair. 1974

"Alone in the Caribbean" by Fenger. 1917

"Lagooned in the Virgin Islands" by Hazel B. Eadie. Pub. Routledge & Sons, Ltd. 1931

"The Blue Book" No.10 Colonial Reports. 1897

"Letters from the Virgin Islands" Anon. Pub. John Van Voorst. 1843

"Records of a Family of Engineers" by RLS Stevenson. Pub. Chatto and Windus. 1912

"Voyage to Windward" by JC Furnas. Pub. Faber and Faber. 1952

The Tortola Public Records Office. Land titles and deeds

Copies of Original Manuscripts and letters. Public Record Office, London. 1750 and 1751

Letter from Juan Bonilla to Marquis de la Ensenada. 11th November, 1750

Confessions during examination of William Blackstock. 26th November, 1750

Extract of letter from Lieutenant Gov. Fleming to the Duke of Bedford. 12th December, 1750

Letter from Juan Bonilla to Marquis de la Ensenada. 15th December, 1750

Letter from Manuel Franco to Gov. Fleming. January, 1971